Magic Blanket Tales

A Child's Mind: Treat with tender
loving care, then soak with a lifetime
of fun and imagination.

For Caitlin Rose

PUBLISHED BY MAGIC BLANKET TALES©
CAMWOOD COURT, EAST MORTON, WEST YORKSHIRE, BD20 5QQ
ENGLAND

Text and illustrations © 2011 by Magic Blanket Tales

First Printing, 2011

ISBN 13: 978 0 9571110 0 4

To learn more about other products from Magic Blanket Tales©, visit us at: www.magicblankettales.co.uk

Printed by: Gold Printing Group Ltd.
www.goldprinting.cc

To Becky
may all your adventures
be giant ones.
Richard x

A MAGIC BLANKET TALES© BOOK

Katie and the Giant Problem

written by **Richard Parr**   illustrated by **Monika Suska**   directed by **Caitlin Rose Parr** (age 7¹/₂)

Today was Katie's 5th birthday. It had been a wonderful princess and pirate party, with a candy filled piñata and the deck made into a pirate ship. The girls played dress up and the boys took turns walking the plank. After all her friends had left, Katie helped clean up the garden. Still dancing and blowing bubbles, she was about to catch the biggest bubble of all when her mother called to her through the open window. "Katie, your Nana's here to see you."

"I'll be right there," Katie replied. Katie turned back just in time to see the biggest bubble land on the grass and disappear. Katie didn't mind. She was always very excited to see her Nana, as she always brought her something very special and today was no exception.

When Katie ran into the living room, there was Nana with her old carpetbag resting on her lap. "What's in the bag Nana? What's in the bag?" Katie said with a very big smile on her face.

"Something I have been waiting to give you for a very long time my darling." Nana opened the bag and pulled out a large quilted blanket, it really wasn't what Katie was expecting as she had quite a few blankets already. Nana could see Katie struggling to look excited about this latest gift, so she turned to Katie's mother and said, "how about a cup of tea?"

"Of course Nana, I'll go and put the kettle on."

Once Katie's mother had left the room, Nana turned to Katie and whispered in her ear, "this is a magic blanket." Katie turned to see a smile on her Nana's face as if she were a little girl herself. "My Grandmother gave me this blanket when I was five and told me to pass it on to my granddaughter when she was five. So how old are you today?"

"Oooh! Five! Five! I'm five years old Nana," Katie said with excitement.

"Then tonight take this blanket and put it on your bed. Now be sure to wait until your mother and father have said goodnight and have gone downstairs, as the magic will only work for you and you alone."

"Do you have a favourite toy?" asked Nana.

"Penny, she always sleeps with me," said Katie. Penny was a soft toy dog, a Dalmatian Katie got on her 3rd birthday and had never left her side except for the occasional ride in the washing machine. And though her coat was no longer white and her left ear was in need of repair, she was Katie's very best friend.

"Good," said Nana. "Make sure Penny is with you under the blanket, you may need a little help when you get there."

"Get there?" asked Katie, "Where Nana?"

"Oh I can't say my dear, it's somewhere new every time."

"You will also need this." Nana reached into the large carpetbag and pulled out a shiny pale blue torch. "No need for batteries," Nana explained, "you just wind the handle."

"Here's what you do. Get under the blanket with Penny and the torch, close your eyes and slowly count to five, and hold on tight to the blanket. Now there is one rule and it is very important. Never stay longer than you need to, when it's time to come home, the torch will start to flash on and off. When it does, hurry and get under the blanket again. Close your eyes, slowly count to five and when you open them you'll be back home in your bed."

Later that evening Katie tidied up her room and put the new blanket on her bed.

She hurried to brush her teeth. She brushed the top and bottom teeth, and then she carefully brushed her very first wobbly tooth that she was very excited about.

Remembering everything Nana told her, Katie made sure the torch was fully charged and grabbed Penny before jumping into bed.

"Would you like a story?" asked Daddy. "Not tonight, thank you. I am very sleepy already and can't wait to try my new blanket. I mean sleep under my new blanket."

"Ok, night night, love you."

"I love you too," Katie replied and she watched as he closed the door but not all the way, Katie always liked it open just a bit to let some light in.

Katie waited a few minutes until she was sure that her parents were downstairs watching television. She crept back from the door and got under the blanket. Holding Penny in one hand and the torch in the other, Katie slid under the blanket and shut her eyes. She began to count "one... two... three... four..." then she held her breath for a moment... "FIVE"

Woooooosssshhhh! Suddenly Katie felt as though she was flying through the air but she did not dare to let go of Penny or open her eyes.

That was until she heard a yelp and looked down to see that Penny was now a real puppy. Katie could hardly believe her eyes. Penny had a very surprised look on her face too.

Then everything stopped. Katie bravely threw off the blanket to reveal a huge forest with the tallest trees she had ever seen and the sun was now coming up.

"I can't believe it," said Katie, looking at Penny. "You're real." Penny began to bark as loud as she could at the tall trees. "What is it Penny?" Katie asked.

Just then they heard a loud roar... "Arrrggggghh!" Then a scream for help and out of the trees ran two woodsmen.

"Run!" they shouted. Katie picked up Penny and began to run but tripped over a rock. One of the woodsmen picked her up and threw her over his shoulder.

Holding tight to Penny and shining the torch towards the trees, Katie could now see what they were running from.

There behind them was a great Big, Humongous GIANT!

He was chasing them and waving his arms around. He roared again. "Arrrggggghh!"

They ran through the trees and into a clearing where a beautiful village stood. The villagers, who were getting ready for market day, had also heard the noise. They were shaken by the giants thundering footsteps and began running in the same direction until they all reached the great Town Hall.

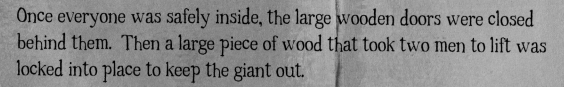

Once everyone was safely inside, the large wooden doors were closed behind them. Then a large piece of wood that took two men to lift was locked into place to keep the giant out.

"You and your dog will be safe in here." Just then they heard the roar again,

"Arrrggggghh!" It was even louder this time.

Katie and Penny looked out of the window and came face to face with the giant looking in. But instead of being scared, Katie just looked back at him and noticed a big tear in his eye.

The giant then turned away and went and sat down next to the big wishing well in the centre of the village. Katie watched as a giant tear ran down his cheek and into the well making a big splash.

"He looks sad," said Katie and Penny nodded in agreement. "This must be why we're here," and with that Katie opened the window and jumped out.

"No! He'll eat you!" the frightened villagers all shouted.

As Katie and Penny approached the giant, another tear rolled off his cheek making a giant puddle around Katie's feet.

Katie looked up and asked the sad giant,
"What's wrong?" The giant looked down
to see Katie and Penny.

He was amazed that they were not
screaming and running away. He wiped
another tear from his cheek and slowly
lifted his left thumb to show it to them.
It was bright red and looked very sore.

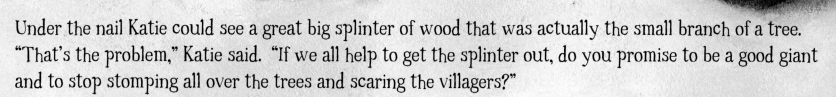

Under the nail Katie could see a great big splinter of wood that was actually the small branch of a tree.
"That's the problem," Katie said. "If we all help to get the splinter out, do you promise to be a good giant
and to stop stomping all over the trees and scaring the villagers?"

"I promise," said the giant.

Katie went back to the Town Hall and knocked on the huge doors. The villagers were still too scared, so Katie stood on her tiptoes and spoke through the letterbox.

She began explaining the problem and how the giant had promised to be good if they helped him. One by one the villagers all slowly emerged from behind the huge doors and followed Katie to the village square.

"How do you expect to get the splinter, I mean branch out?," asked one of the villagers in a nervous voice.

Just then Penny began to bark and then jumped up onto the wall of the well. "Of course," said Katie. "We can use the rope from the well. Good idea Penny!" Katie tied one end of the rope around the branch.

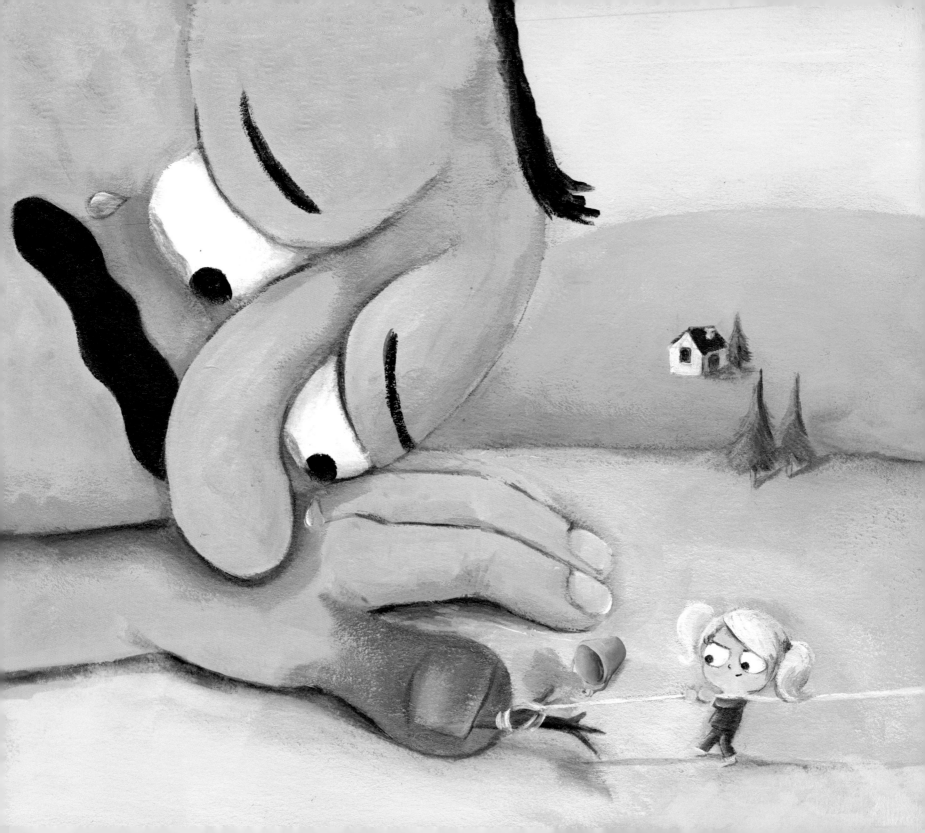

"Now it's going to take all of us to get the branch out," Katie explained. So the villagers all lined up, women and children too. Katie held on at the front and Penny took hold of the other end with her teeth.

"Ok everyone, pull!" Katie shouted, "Pull!" So, they all pulled with all their might.

The giant let out another great roar. "Arrrggggghh!" and even though they were still a bit scared, they kept on pulling, until finally with a crunching crashing sound, out it came.

"Hurray!" They all shouted and celebrated by throwing their hats into the air. A great big smile appeared on the giants face.

"Oh! Thank you, that feels so much better," he said taking a deep breath.

The giant then stood up, and in front of everyone promised, that from this day forward he would be their friend and help them in any way he could.

Everyone cheered again and even more hats flew into the air. Just then Katie noticed the torch begin to flash. Penny also noticed and barked at it.

Remembering what her Nana had said, Katie said she was sorry but she must be on her way.

The giant asked if he could help. "Yes, can you get Penny and I back to the forest as quickly as you can? I need to find my blanket and I don't know the way back."

The giant lifted Katie and Penny up in his hand that did not hurt anymore and placed them into his shirt pocket. Katie and Penny waved goodbye to everyone.

The giant then turned and took several large but careful steps back through the forest to the small opening, where on the ground lay Katie's magic blanket.

The giant lifted Katie and Penny out of his shirt pocket and carefully lowered them to the ground. Katie thanked the giant and reminded him to keep his promise to be good and kind to all the villagers. The giant nodded, then he turned and headed home.

Katie and Penny both climbed under the blanket and Katie pulled it over their heads. "Ready Penny?" Katie asked.

"Ruff! Ruff!" barked Penny, wagging her tail.

Katie began to count "one... two... three... four..."

This time they both held their breath for a moment... "FIVE."

Once again Katie felt like she was flying through the air and held onto Penny even tighter than before.

When all was quiet, Katie pulled back the blanket and just as Nana had promised, she was back in her own cozy bed.

Just then, Katie saw her bedroom door open and her mother slowly leaned in and asked. "Are you alright? It sounded like there was a giant stomping around up here."

Katie just smiled, "No, it's just me and Penny," she replied.

Looking down, Katie could see Penny was back to her old self, a well worn, but well loved soft toy. Katie turned over and cuddling into Penny she whispered, "I can't wait until our next adventure." Then she closed her eyes and fell fast asleep.

The End, or perhaps it's just the beginning...

Magic Blanket Tales

A Child's Mind: Treat with tender loving care, then soak with a lifetime of fun and imagination.